AND THEN IT HAPPENED

·· 12 ··

M & L Wade

Books for Boys

ISBN 9780988115217

Printed in Canada by Hignell Book Printing

Books For Boys Inc.
P.O. Box 87
Strathroy ON N7G 3J1

Table of Contents

Chapter 1

Vegas!

It was a hot Friday afternoon at the beginning of summer. Paulo and I were spending a few days at Gordon's house while our parents were away on vacation. It had been a *boring* few days since Gordon was grounded after bringing home a disappointing report card at the end of June. According to his report card, with just a little effort, Gordon could be at the top of the class. Instead, he put all his effort into thinking up new ways to get out of doing homework, and he avoided studying for tests altogether. Gordon's parents thought that grounding him would do him some good, but all it did was give Gordon time to write report cards on his mother and father's parenting skills. Sadly, it turned out that both his parents were getting failing grades. Gordon, however, felt that with just a little more effort, his parents could be outstanding. He suggested they celebrate "Gordon Day," or even "Gordon Week," to bump up their marks and improve their parenting skills at the same time. Paulo and I couldn't wait to see his parents' reactions to their report cards, especially after a long, tiring week of work.

When Gordon's parents arrived home, they both jumped out of the car yelling, "WE JUST WON A *FREE* 3-DAY VACATION FOR TWO IN LAS VEGAS! WHOO-HOO! AND ALL FOR BEING THE 100,000[TH] CAR TO DRIVE THROUGH THE CAR WASH!!"

Gordon quietly slipped the report cards into his pockets. He was interested in hearing more of this new development.

"What about us kids?" Gordon asked. "What happens to us?"

"Well," his mother answered. "I phoned my sister and she was happy to take the girls, but she doesn't have enough beds for you boys. She sends you her love, though. Funny thing is, I must have phoned a dozen other friends and relatives. As soon as I mentioned babysitting you three boys, they all remembered that they didn't have enough spare beds. But they all send you their love."

Hmmm, I thought to myself. *Gordon's relatives need a little less love and a lot more beds.*

"So," Gordon's dad said, "we decided to take you boys with us to Las Vegas!"

Gordon, Paulo and I jumped to our feet and cheered. Three days in Vegas, three boys...What could possibly go wrong?

The next morning our plane touched down in Las Vegas and we found a limousine waiting to take us to our hotel. As we rode through the city, we stared at the huge hotels, the casinos and the crowds of people. The limousine drove on and we left the lights and crowds behind us, finally coming to a stop at a place where the hotels were much smaller and not nearly as fancy.

"Everybody out!" called the limo driver. "We're here." We stared up at a faded sign that read, 'Good Fellas Hotel.'

"Well," said Mrs. Smith. "This seems nice enough. And it *is* a free trip."

"It'll be fine," said Mr. Smith, grabbing the suitcases. "We're in Vegas, and we're here for fun! Hey, boys, how about if you explore a little while your mother and I take a nap in the hotel room. It's been a long trip."

"Yes," agreed Mrs. Smith, looking around. "Freemont Street. That sounds like a nice, safe place for you boys to explore. How about if you meet us back here in a couple of hours and we'll get some dinner then?"

Gordon, Paulo and I looked at each other. They were leaving us alone in Las Vegas? What kind of parents did that? And why couldn't I have that kind of parents?

"Yes!" we agreed quickly.

"Great! See you in a couple of hours. Better make it three," said Mr. Smith, and Gordon's parents rushed into the hotel, leaving us standing alone on the sidewalk.

"Just another example of poor parenting," Gordon sighed. "First they take three boys to Las Vegas, and now they're leaving us on the street alone."

"Yeah," I agreed. "We could get into all kinds of trouble in a town like this."

A slow grin spread across Gordon's face. "You're right!" he said. "I'll bet we could. In fact, I'm sure of it. My parents really messed up this time. They're trusting us alone for a few hours in Las Vegas. This kind of poor parenting has got to stop, for their own sake."

"Right," said Paulo. "If they keep going down this path, there's no telling *how* you'll turn out."

"Let's start with a yelling contest," suggested Gordon. "That's sure to attract some attention." Gordon started yelling at the top of his lungs, and Paulo and I joined in. In no time at all, a crowd had gathered around us.

"What are you kids doing?" asked a man with a drink in his hand.

"We're having a yelling contest," explained Gordon.

"Great!" shouted the man, pulling some bills out of his pocket. "I got five dollars on the short kid!" Money suddenly appeared and bets were made as a crowd gathered and listened to Gordon, Paulo and me as we yelled and shouted until we were hoarse. Money

5

exchanged hands. The winners collected their piles and a few people gave the three of us some money as well for providing some gambling entertainment.

"Thanks, boys!" the crowd said as they wandered away. "That was a lot of fun."

Gordon, Paulo and I stared open-mouthed at the money in our hands. "I guess it takes more than that to get into trouble in Las Vegas," I said.

"We'll see about that," said Gordon, and he ran over to a nearby garbage can and shouted, "I'm gonna lift this garbage can over my head and throw it onto the street!"

"Hey!" yelled a woman. "This kid's gonna throw a garbage can onto the street!"

"I'll bet he can't even lift it," said a man beside her. "I'll bet ten bucks on it!" Once again, a crowd gathered around Gordon and bets were quickly placed. "Okay, kid, give it your best shot!" yelled a man.

Gordon picked up the heavy garbage can, heaved it over his head, and threw it onto the street. A roar went up from the crowd and the winners cheered and gathered up their money. Dollar bills were thrust into Gordon's hands.

"You can't do *anything* wrong in this town," said Paulo in amazement.

"I'll bet fighting is illegal," said Gordon. "Let's pretend to get into a huge fight!"

The three of us tackled each other and rolled around on the street, throwing fake punches and kicks. Immediately, another crowd gathered around us, chanting, cheering and placing bets. After a few minutes of 'fighting,' Gordon, Paulo and I were exhausted and lay on the ground panting and gasping for air. Suddenly a shadow loomed over us and we opened our eyes to see three big policemen. They reached down and grabbed us by our arms, picking us up and standing us on our feet.

"Boys," said the sergeant, "I just want to say that was the best fight I've seen all day. Well done!" They patted us on the back and disappeared into the crowd.

Adding up all of our money, Gordon said, "Hey! Let's go into the hotel casino and try gambling! What can we lose?"

We walked through the hotel lobby but we were stopped at the entrance to the casino by a security guard. "No kids allowed," he said.

"Darn! What's there to do in this hotel for kids?" Gordon asked.

"Not much here except gambling," the security guard answered. "But there's a free gangster museum in the lower level. Some kids seem to like that."

We headed for the museum. It was full of famous gangsters from the early days of Las Vegas, all life-size, realistic wax models, fully dressed in old-style gangster clothing. It was here that Gordon got his next great idea.

"Hey, guys," he said. "Let's go back upstairs and try gambling."

That's impossible," said Paulo. "Security's already stopped us."

"Ahh, *we've* been kicked out, but three old men haven't been kicked out," replied Gordon with a sly grin. "Quick! Grab these clothes and wigs off the wax dummies and get changed," said Gordon.

Ten minutes later, three old men wearing gangster-style suits headed into the casino, right past security.

As our eyes adjusted to the dark casino, we found a game that looked interesting and not too difficult. We watched for a few minutes. It was called Roulette, and it seemed that all you had to do was pick a number, place your money on it, and wait for a little ball to spin around a wheel and come to rest on a number. If that number matched the number you picked, you won! This game was called 'Ten To One' because today, they were giving you ten times your money if you actually won.

"That's probably because nobody ever wins," said Paulo.

"I'm going to try it anyway," insisted Gordon, and he placed all of our money, $100.00, on a red number 17. The dealer spun the wheel around, and we waited for it to slow down and for the little ball to come to a rest. We couldn't believe our eyes!

"17 Red!" called out the dealer. "Winner! $1000.00" He pointed to Gordon. "Do you wish to play again?"

"YES!" shrieked Gordon. And then, remembering what he'd heard some other players saying, he said, "Let it ride!" This meant that he was going to play the same number again, and with all the money he'd just won.

"Are you crazy?" I hissed. "You're going to lose everything we just won!"

The dealer spun the wheel again, and the little ball went around and around. As it slowed down, the little ball bounced to a stop.

"17 Red!" called out the dealer again, sounding excited. "$10,000.00!"

The money was really piling up. Gordon had now won ten thousand dollars! "Let it ride!" he called again, getting caught up in the excitement. A small crowd of interested gamblers gathered around Gordon.

For a third unbelievable time, the little ball came to a rest on number 17 red! There was a buzz in the casino and the crowd around Gordon grew larger. He had now won $100,000!! People cheered and yelled like it was New Year's Eve.

"Well," asked the dealer. "Are you going to quit while you're ahead, or try for an amazing *one million dollars*?"

And then it happened. Just as Gordon drew a deep breath to yell "Let it ride!" his fake moustache came loose and he swallowed it. He began coughing so hard that his wig fell off his head and landed on the Roulette table. In an instant, two huge, muscular security guards were on him. Four more appeared from out of nowhere and grabbed Paulo and me. They ripped off our wigs and moustaches. Gordon, Paulo and I were suspended in the air, a guard holding onto each side of us.

Next, a very well-dressed man approached. The man was huge. He wore heavy gold rings on each finger, and his nose was bent to one side as though he had been in more than a few fights.

"Well, well, well," he said in a low raspy voice. "A bunch of wise guys who think they can steal from my casino wearing my dear sweet dead grampa's clothing. You should be ashamed of yourselves."

At that moment, Gordon's parents entered the casino. Catching sight of the three of us being held up in the air,

Gordon's mother let out a shriek. The casino owner turned and said, "Who are you?"

"We're the parents!" she yelled.

"Well, where I come from, parents are responsible for their kids, and yours are breaking at least thirty state gambling laws. Parents like you give Vegas a bad name. Your parenting skills disgust me!"

All the gamblers in the casino put down their drinks and ground out their cigarettes. They folded their arms and looked down their noses at Gordon's parents.

"Now, I want you and your kids out of my hotel. In fact, I'm banning you from *all* the hotels in Vegas. Now get on a plane and go back home, if you know what's good for you."

It was a very, very quiet flight home. No one spoke. Hours later, as Gordon's dad pulled into the driveway, Gordon pulled his parents' report cards out of his pocket and whispered to Paulo and me, "Do you think this is a good time to give these to them?"

Chapter 2

The World's Oldest Teacher

It was recess and Gordon, Paulo and I were outside sitting against the school wall with library books in our hands. We looked like the best kids in the whole school. In fact, we were the *worst* kids in the school! You see, we had recently discovered that if we sat quietly under the open window of the principal's office, we could secretly listen to all of his private conversations and telephone calls. So far we had learned that he was supposed to bring home a loaf of bread and that he had a dentist appointment in two weeks. It turned out that our principal is a very boring man. Just as we were about to give up and play some soccer, we heard a knock on the door and then the very happy voice of our teacher.

13

"Oh, Mr. Evans. I'm glad I caught you in the office."

"You sure seem happy today," he replied suspiciously.

"Oh, I am happy. It's not every day that I get to give you one of these."

"Oh, no. What is it?" Mr. Evans groaned.

"A note from my doctor saying that I am to have a week off work for a little operation," she said smugly.

"No! No! Not that! Anything but that!" cried Mr. Evans. "You know I'll never find a supply teacher to cover your class for an entire week! Why don't you just wait for summer break to have the operation?"

That must have been a private joke between them, because Mrs. H. instantly burst out laughing. "During the summer?" she gasped. "*During the summer?* Ha! Ha! Ha! Stop it! You're killing me!"

As Mrs. Hoagsbrith's laughter died away, we could hear Mr. Evans muttering to himself. "Oh, dear. What am I going to do? I'll never find a supply teacher for that class. The last one I got left the country, and the one before her took early retirement. If I can't find someone to cover her class, then I'm going to have to give the kids the week off."

Gordon, Paulo and I jumped to our feet and raced to tell the other kids in our class the great news! When the bell rang to end recess, our teacher watched in puzzlement as our class formed a conga line and danced our way down the hall to our classroom.

For the rest of the day and all weekend, it was all we talked about. Would Mr. Evans be able to find a teacher to cover our class next week or wouldn't he?

On Monday morning, we arrived at school early and waited anxiously by the parking lot to spot any unfamiliar cars. No one arrived that we didn't know. When the bell rang, we rushed to our classroom to wait for Mr. Evans to come and send us home for the week. Sure enough, at nine o'clock, the principal appeared at our door and said, "Class, I have great news!"

Instantly everyone began cheering! Confetti filled the air and kids blew party horns.

"Yes," Mr. Evans continued, holding up his hands for silence. "I'm as happy about it as you are. I searched all weekend and I finally found a supply teacher to take on this class for the entire week!" Looking out the window, he said, "Ah, and here comes your supply teacher now."

Disappointed, we turned to the window and saw a small car slowly pull into the parking lot. It slowly backed into a parking space and after a few minutes, the door slowly swung open. Our mouths opened in shock as an old man of about 70 slowly got out of the car and stood bent over, leaning on a cane. We turned back to our principal and Gordon said, "You've got to be kidding! That can't be our teacher!"

"Of course not," chuckled Mr. Evans. "That man isn't even a teacher. But his mother is!"

Our heads swung back to the window at once, and we watched as the old man shuffled around to the other side of the car and opened the door. And then it happened. Very, very slowly, he helped an ancient woman out of the car and then took a walker out of the back seat for her. She was 95 years old if she was a day! We stared as she made her way across the parking lot, stopping to rest every now and then.

"Yup," Mr. Evans smiled. "She's perfect, isn't she? I looked for a teacher for a hundred miles in all directions and came up empty handed. I nearly had to send you kids home for the week, but then I stumbled onto this one in an old age home. She's been retired for 40 years but she says she's *rarin' to go!*"

Rarin' to go where? I wondered as I watched her take four steps and stop to catch her breath.

When she finally got to the classroom twenty minutes later, she shuffled right up to the row of coats at the back of the room and said, "Hello, class. My name is Mrs. Johnson."

Mr. Evans hurried over to her and spun her around. "Well, now, Mrs. Johnson. It looks like you have things well under control. I'll be in my office if you need me." And he quickly scurried out of the room.

Mrs. Johnson made her way to the teacher's desk, sat down and smiled at us. Then she tilted her head back and fell asleep. For the first time ever, our class didn't know what to do. We had a 95 year-old teacher, and she was snoring away at the front of the room!

"Quiet," Gordon whispered. "Let the old girl sleep." For the next hour, we quietly chatted and played computer games. At 10:30, the recess bell rang, waking Mrs. Johnson with a start.

"What on earth was that?" she exclaimed.

"The recess bell," we told her.

"Oh, recess. I'm going to pass. You all go on without me. Have a great time." And she promptly fell back asleep.

During recess, we decided that maybe old Mrs. Johnson wasn't so bad after all. At least she wasn't working us too hard, and she hadn't yelled at anyone all morning.

Coming in after recess, our supply teacher was nowhere in sight. But much to Gordon's delight, his set of fake plastic teeth that Mrs. Hoagsbrith had confiscated two months ago was sitting on the teacher's desk.

"Great!" said Gordon, grabbing the teeth and popping them into his mouth. For the next ten minutes he entertained us with funny faces and silly grins.

Finally, the door opened and Mrs. Johnson shuffled over to the teacher's desk. She stopped and looked at the desk, and then slowly turned around to face us.

"Hath anyone theen my falth teeth?" she lisped, pointing to the desk. "I could have thworn I left them right here."

Gordon turned white as a sheet and fainted. Gasping with laughter, I grabbed the teeth from his mouth and handed them to Mrs. Johnson. "These must be them," I said.

"Oh, thank you!" she said, popping them into her mouth. "Wait. What's that on your face?"

Before I could move, she grabbed me with one hand and pulled a lace hanky out of her pocket with the other. Spitting on the hanky, she began wiping dirt off my face. Then she noticed the girl beside me, whose hair was windblown and tangled from recess. Spitting on her hand, she ran it over the girl's hair to smooth it down. Terrified of being spat on, the rest of the class quickly began smoothing their own hair and brushing dirt and crumbs off their faces.

Once everyone had settled down, Mrs. Johnson sat down, smiled, and fell asleep. She snored quietly until the lunch bell rang.

Scared of getting dirty or windblown, our class huddled next to the school doors outside and discussed our situation.

"Well," said Gordon, "on the one hand, she's kind and doesn't make us do any work. But on the other hand, she spits on us! Let's have a vote. Who wants to keep the old girl?"

No one said anything.

"Well, who wants to get rid of her?" he asked. Every hand went up. It was unanimous. The only problem was *how do you get rid of a 95 year-old teacher?*

It turns out, getting rid of Mrs. Johnson was easier than we thought. Gordon came up with a brilliant plan. Sneaking into school early the next day, Gordon put on a flowered dress and a wig that he had worn for Halloween one year when he dressed up like our teacher. He stood by the window and waited. Paulo and I waited in the parking lot. When Mrs. Johnson and her son pulled in,

Paulo and I were ready. We went quickly over to the car and pointed to our classroom window. We explained that Mrs. Hoagsbrith had made a remarkable recovery and she was already back at work. We no longer needed a supply teacher. Gordon waved from the classroom window. Mrs. Johnson looked up at the window, gave a sad little smiled and sighed. "Well, it was fun while it lasted," she said. "I'll miss you all. You are a dear group of boys and girls." She and her son drove off.

We posted a sign on our classroom door that read "Shh. Do Not Disturb. Testing." For the rest of the week, we watched movies, played video games and listened to music. It was the best week we ever had!

The following Monday, Mrs. Hoagsbrith returned to school. "Mr. Evans told me that your class had testing all last week," she said. "I'm so sorry. I think that you kids deserve a break today, so we are not going to do any work at all! Instead, we are going to watch movies and play computer games!"

It was good to have our teacher back.

Chapter 3

A Free Lunch

One of the girls in our class, Alex, lives across the street from Gordon. Her parents own a bike store in town, and for her last birthday, they gave Alex a new racing bike. She is now the fastest cyclist in our school. I've noticed that when a comic book character has a special super power, that power can be used for good or evil. Alex decided to use her super racing power for pure evil.

Lately, Alex had taken to jumping on her bike immediately after school and racing over to Gordon's house to tell Mrs. Smith everything inappropriate that Gordon had said or done at school that day. When

Gordon would arrive home, many minutes later, his mom would meet him in the driveway with a snarl on her face, and things would only get worse from there. Gordon usually ended up in his room waiting for his father to get home.

On this particular day, however, I returned from school to see Alex and her fast bike leaving *my* house, and it was *my* mother who was standing outside waiting to greet *me*. She didn't even wait for me to reach the driveway before she started yelling. "Well, I heard all about your behaviour today! You go straight to your room and wait for your father to get home!! Just wait until I tell him what you've been up to!"

If Gordon and I thought we had it rough, things were much worse for poor Paulo. The day after she visited my house, Alex paid a visit to Paulo's house after school. Unfortunately for Paulo, his father happened to be at home when Alex reached the Lima's farm. When Paulo got off the bus, he saw Alex sitting on her bike talking to his dad in the doorway of the barn. Mr. Lima was holding a pitch fork and he kept slapping the handle against his palm as Alex talked. Noticing Paulo approaching, Alex smiled, said good-bye to Mr. Lima, and raced off on her bike.

To Paulo's surprise, Mr. Lima didn't yell and demand to hear Paulo's side of the story. He simply handed the pitch fork to Paulo and said, "I hear you were sent to the principal's office today for playing too rough at recess. That must mean that you have too much energy for your own good. Perhaps it would help you burn off some of this energy if you were to do all of *my* farm chores before starting your own. You should be done by 11, midnight at the latest, just in time to start your homework."

So now, thanks to Alex, Gordon, Paulo and I had to be on our best behaviour at school. At the tiniest sign of trouble, Alex would jump on her bike and pedal off to tell our parents faster than we could say, "We didn't do it!"

"What I don't get," said Gordon one day at recess, "is what Alex has to gain by ratting us out."

"Maybe she just doesn't like us," I suggested.

"That's crazy!" exclaimed Gordon. "What's not to like?"

Just then we saw our principal come out of the building with a bucket and a rag. Mr. Evans headed straight over to the bike rack. We watched as he oiled the chain on Alex's bike and then pumped up her tires. Then he began waxing her bike!

"So that's it!" said Paulo. "What a little sneak!"

"I can't believe she'd do this to us!" said Gordon.

"What?" I asked. "Who's doing *what* to us?"

"Don't you see?" explained Paulo. "Mr. Evans and Alex have struck some kind of deal. In exchange for Alex telling our parents what we've been up to at school every day, Mr. Evans cleans her bike and oils the chain and all that. That way, Mr. Evans doesn't have to worry about us getting into trouble at school because he knows that our parents will find out exactly what we've been up to, thanks to Alex and her fast bike!"

"That little sneak!" I said. "Gordon, you've got to do something!"

"Just give me a little time," said Gordon. "I'll think of something to get Alex back."

Paulo and I smiled knowing it would be something good…very good indeed.

* * * * *

Three days later, Gordon came up to Paulo and me and said, "Guys, I think I've finally found a way to get back at Alex." He told us his plan…

* * * * *

On Saturday morning, Gordon, Paulo and I sat on Gordon's front porch and watched as Alex's parents got in their car and drove to their bike store for the day. The three of us then went shopping. When we returned, we crossed the street and knocked on Alex's front door. Moments later, the door was opened by Alex. Her smile changed to a frown when she saw us standing on her porch.

"Oh, it's *you*," she said sourly. "What do you want?"

"Can we come in for a minute?" asked Paulo.

"Absolutely not!" shouted Alex. "My parents don't allow me to have boys in the house, especially when they're not home. And ESPECIALLY not you three!"

"Well," said Gordon. "We're in kind of a jam, and we really could use your help. Our parents have all gone away for the day, and we're supposed to look after ourselves. Cook, and make lunch, and all that. They even left us grocery money." Gordon reached into his pocket and pulled out a wad of money. Dramatically, he fanned it out for Alex to see. "They left us $200.00 for food and emergencies. The problem is," he continued, "that we don't know how to cook, and we remember those great cookies you made us when you first moved in."

"And we were wondering," said Paulo, "if you'd mind making us some more of those wonderful cookies, and then maybe making us lunch."

"And dinner!" I added. "We'll pay you all the money our parents left us."

Alex narrowed her eyes. "All of it? $200.00? Just for cooking and baking for you for one day?"

"That's right," said Gordon. Alex continued to glare at us, but I could tell she was thinking it over. Gordon held the money a little closer to her and she reached for it.

27

"Not so fast," said Gordon. "First you have to cook for us, and then we'll pay you."

"Okay," she said. "Get in here, quick, before somebody sees you and tells my parents."

"Thanks, Alex," said Gordon. "You won't regret this."

"I'd better not. And you can't breathe a word of this to my parents."

"Of course not," said Paulo. "We wouldn't dream of snitching on you. Now how about if we watch some TV while you bake us a big batch of those delicious cookies?"

"Alright" said Alex. "The TV's in there, and I'll go into the kitchen and get started."

For the next hour, Gordon, Paulo and I watched TV while Alex worked hard in the kitchen. The delicious smell of cookies wafted into the living room as Alex appeared at the door with a tray piled high with chocolate chip cookies and three tall glasses of milk. We munched away while Alex cleaned up the mess in the kitchen.

When she finally finished, Gordon wandered into the kitchen and said, "So, what's for lunch?"

"Lunch?" frowned Alex. "You can't possibly be hungry after eating all those cookies!"

"We're growing boys," said Gordon. "And we'd love some burgers and fries. Or maybe some tacos. But you probably don't know how to make tacos."

"Of course I know how to make tacos!" Alex huffed. "Now get out of my kitchen while I get to work!"

We stretched out in the living room while Alex set to work making us tacos for lunch. Finally she yelled, "Come and get it!" The tacos were delicious, but the kitchen was a mess, and Alex had to spend another hour cleaning it up. By then, of course, we were hungry again.

"Hey, Alex!" shouted Gordon. "How about a little snack?"

"What?" she shrieked. "You cannot possibly still be hungry!"

"But we are," I replied. "And we *are* paying you $200.00."

"Oh, all right!" said Alex, stomping back into the kitchen.

We kept her busy cooking and waiting on us until nearly five o'clock. When she finally cleaned up the kitchen for the last time, we thanked her and headed for the front door.

"Here's the $200.00 we promised you," said Gordon, handing it to Alex as we headed home.

"Remember!" she called after us, running out onto the porch. "No one can know you were here today. My parents will kill me if they knew I let you in."

"Don't worry," we said. "You can trust *us*!"

We slowly crossed the street to Gordon's house, and just as we were almost there, a car pulled into Alex's driveway. Her father jumped out and saw Alex standing on the front porch.

"Did I just see Gordon and his two friends leaving here?" he demanded.

"Ahh, I can explain, dad," replied Alex meekly. And then it happened.

"Good," said her father without waiting for Alex to continue. He held out his hand. "Gordon was at my store this morning and he bought a new bike. He said he'd bring the money over this afternoon and leave it with you."

Speechless, Alex reached into her pocket and handed over the money, glaring at Gordon, Paulo and me across the street.

Chapter 4

Danger Pay

It was February. For weeks our class had been looking forward to going on a tubing field trip at a ski resort several hours outside of town. Our teacher, Mrs. Hoagsbrith, had chosen this particular ski resort because not only did it have the best tubing hills, but it was a French-speaking resort. She said we could all work on our French skills while having a great time. "Even I'm looking forward to this trip," she said.

Two days before the field trip, however, Mrs. H. developed a cold. We all noticed her sniffling and coughing. Gordon was the first to show his concern.

"Maybe you should take tomorrow off so you'll be better for our trip on Friday," he said. "We wouldn't, I mean, *you* wouldn't want to miss this one. You said so yourself."

The next day, Mrs. Hoagsbrith arrived at school as usual, but she looked even worse than the day before. She could hardly talk and she was feverish.

"You should have stayed home and gotten a supply teacher today," said Gordon. Despite her illness, Mrs. Hoagsbrith scoffed.

"Easier said than done. I tried 5 supply teachers this morning, and they were all busy. At least that's what they said. Don't worry. I'm sure I'll be better by tomorrow. The trip won't be cancelled."

But on Friday morning when we entered our room, Mrs. Hoagsbrith was nowhere to be seen.

"Oh, no!" moaned Paulo. "There goes our great trip."

Suddenly, Mrs. Hoagsbrith staggered into the classroom. "Here I am. Sorry I'm late, but I'm even worse today. I'm afraid we're going to have to cancel our trip to the ski resort."

"What?" exclaimed Gordon. "Why can't we get a supply teacher to take us?"

"I tried to find a supply teacher, but they all laughed and said, *'Take your class on a field trip? Ha! Ha! Ha! Does it come with danger pay? Sorry, I'm busy today.'* Then they hung up."

"I can't believe this," said a voice at the door. We all turned and saw our principal, Mr. Evans, standing there. "Mrs. Hoagsbrith, you look terrible. What are you doing out of bed? I can't believe you couldn't get a supply teacher! And what do they mean, *danger pay?* I think it's time I showed all these teachers a thing or two about classroom supervision. Kids, get your gear together. *I'm* taking you on this field trip, and I don't require danger pay! My motto is: There are no bad classes, only bad teachers, and I'll prove it!!"

We all cheered and grabbed our backpacks and headed for the door. Mrs. Hoagsbrith just stared at Mr. Evans. "Well, don't say I didn't warn you," she said between sniffles.

"Nonsense!" said Mr. Evans. "What could possibly go wrong? The kids will be just fine."

"It's not the kids I'm worried about," she warned.

*   *   *   *   *

Once outside, Mr. Evans made us line up and promise to be on our best behaviour. He said he wanted to show everyone, even Mrs. H., just how easy it was to manage our class. Then we climbed aboard the waiting bus. To our delight, it was a brand new school bus, shiny and clean.

"Ahhh, that new bus smell," said Mr. Evans, inhaling deeply. "No wet snowsuit and stale lunch smell."

In a couple of hours, we arrived at the French ski resort. Before we got off the bus, we had to promise again to be on our best behaviour.

"This field trip is going to be perfect," said Mr. Evans. "I'm counting on each and every one of you to make me look good."

After two hours on a bus, everyone needed to use the washroom.

"Where are the washrooms?" asked Gordon, looking around.

"We are at a French ski resort so that you can improve your French. En français, Gordon," scolded Mr. Evans. "I believe the proper word is *les toilettes*. Ah, there it is," he said, pointing to a sign.

We all nodded and headed toward the sign. When we were done, Gordon asked eagerly, "Okay, which way to the tubing hills?"

"En français," scolded Mr. Evans again. He pointed at another sign. "*Plente de tubing* is that way." We all quickly dashed off in the direction of the tubing hills.

The next few hours flew by as we tubed down the hills and climbed back to the top over and over again. We were having such a great time that none of us even thought about getting into trouble at all. We just kept sliding down the hills and climbing back up for more fun. Mr. Evans stood at the bottom of the hill, watching. After a couple of hours, he told us he was getting cold just standing around and that he was going to sit in the bus for a few minutes to warm up. Besides, he said, we were all behaving so well that he knew he could trust us alone for a little while.

We charged back up the hill a few more times until finally I said, "I'm starting to get hungry." Everyone agreed that it was time for lunch.

"But where do we eat lunch?" I asked.

"En français," scolded Gordon, in his best imitation of our principal. Then he pointed to a snow-covered sign that said '*LANCH.*' "That must be French for 'lunch,' " said Gordon. "Let's go!"

We all nodded and followed Gordon in the direction of the sign, which pointed up one of the biggest hills. Unfortunately for us, none of us noticed that the blowing snow had covered up most of the sign. Hidden underneath the snow were the words 'EXTREME DANGER. AVALANCHE RISK.'

Our class continued to climb and climb, following the direction of the arrow on the sign.

"The restaurant must be at the top of this hill," said Gordon. But when we got to the top, there was nothing there. We made our way to the edge of the mountain and looked down.

"Cool! You can see the whole resort from here," said Paulo.

"Look! There's Mr. Evans, getting off the bus," observed Gordon.

Mr. Evans climbed down the bus steps and looked around at the tubing hills, no doubt expecting to find us.

"I'll bet he's worried we've gone off and gotten into some kind of trouble," said Gordon. "Let's show him how well we're behaving. Everybody, wave and call out his name!"

"HELLOOOO!" we all yelled. "WE'RE UP HERE, MR. EVANS!" We waved and shouted and jumped up and down. And then it happened. Our jumping and yelling triggered an enormous chunk of snow to break loose and slide down the mountainside, straight toward the parking lot and Mr. Evans! Our principal heard the rumble of the snow and looked up to see what looked like half the mountain racing towards him! He ran for the bus and dove aboard, just as the wall of snow slammed into it, flipping the bus over and burying it with our principal on board!

"Uh-oh," said Gordon quietly. "I hate when that happens. Follow me." We quickly ran back the way we'd come and made it to the bottom of the mountain in time to see a crew of emergency workers digging out our brand new school bus. A few minutes later, Mr. Evans appeared, bumped and bruised, but otherwise unharmed. The bus, however, was totalled!

"Our new bus!" he exclaimed in shock. "Look what happened to our beautiful new bus! And what will your teacher say when she hears about this?"

"That's easy," said Gordon. "She'll say you should have got danger pay!"

Chapter 5

Break-In!

Every spring, the students in our school are given a week-long test. Every subject is covered, except of course for the fun ones like art and gym. We spend hours on math, reading, geography, French and science. We are given page after page of questions to answer while our teachers sit at their desks enjoying the silence while we students slave away. This year was different, however. For the first time, we were to type our answers into the computer so that our tests could be automatically marked. Day after day, we sat at the computers, typing our answers, and by Friday afternoon, our backs were sore and stiff and our fingers were numb from typing.

"Man, am I ever glad that's over," complained Gordon as we left school for the weekend.

"Yeah," agreed Paulo. "I thought writing down all of our answers was bad enough. It's ten times worse on the computer!"

"Well, at least we have a whole weekend with no homework to look forward to," I said. "You guys want to come over and play computer games?"

"Computers? NO WAY!" shouted Gordon and Paulo together.

"I'm not going near a computer for a month," added Paulo. Instead, we spent the weekend riding our bikes, fishing, and watching movies in Gordon's basement. By the time Monday morning came, we had almost forgotten the ordeal of the week before.

Arriving at school that morning, we were surprised to see that one of the windows on the ground floor had been boarded up, and the custodians were outside sweeping up bits of broken glass.

"That's odd," I said. "What do you think happened?"

"I'll bet some kid kicked a soccer ball through the window," said Gordon.

The bell rang, and we entered our classroom. Mr. Evans' voice came over the PA system with the morning announcements. "I'm very sorry to report that we've had a break-in over the weekend. A thief stole all of the school's computers." He paused, as if deciding what to say next. "I hate to tell everyone this, but last week's test answers were on those computers, and without the computers, we have no way of grading your tests. The school board has kindly loaned us some computers and they were busy all weekend setting them up. I'm afraid that you will all have to be tested again this week."

We sat in stunned silence. After a long, miserable week of testing, the last thing anyone wanted was another long, miserable week of *more* testing.

"Well, class," said Mrs. Hoagsbrith, a bit too cheerfully, "I guess we should get started." With a loud groan, we began another week of testing.

The days dragged by until Friday finally arrived. To celebrate finishing our second full week of testing,

Gordon, Paulo and I spent Friday evening at the local ice cream parlour, stuffing ourselves with chocolate sundaes. It was dark outside as we pedaled back to Gordon's house.

As we rode by our school, we noticed a light on in the library on the second floor. We slammed on our brakes and turned off our bike lights. We watched in silence as a shadowy figure walked past a window carrying something that looked suspiciously like a computer.

"Look," whispered Gordon, pointing to an open window on the ground floor. "It must be the computer thief! He's come back!"

We stood in the school yard, watching as the thief walked by the window with another computer. Then it dawned on us. If the thief stole all the computers again, we would be faced with yet *another* week of testing! Gordon, Paulo and I looked at each other, and we knew what we had to do. The fear of a third week of testing was stronger than our fear of the thief. We crawled through the open window of the school and prepared to do battle!

"What we need is a plan," I whispered nervously. Paulo and I both looked at Gordon. After a few seconds,

Gordon smiled and whispered, "Boys, this is going to be fun. Follow me!"

Gordon led us straight to the gym. "We'll set our trap in here," he explained. "And then we'll lure the thief down to the gym and nab him!"

As usual, Gordon had come up with a great plan. The gym was full of things that we could use to catch a thief. It took less than five minutes to get ready and put our plan into action.

Tiptoeing to the bottom of the stairs, Gordon yelled, "Hey, you! Down here!" Then he raced back to the gym, where Paulo and I crouched in the darkness, ready for action. Gordon quickly scampered to the top of the climbers and waited. Within seconds we could hear footsteps heading straight towards the gym!

In the next instant, a large shadow filled the doorframe, and the thief fumbled for the light switch, which we had cleverly hidden behind a bunch of mats.

"Hey! Up here!" yelled Gordon.

"Who said that?" shouted the thief, stepping into the dark gym and walking toward Gordon's voice. "Where are you?"

"Right here!!" yelled Gordon. Shouting like Tarzan, he swung across the gym on a climbing rope, smashing feet-first into the thief's stomach, toppling him over and knocking the wind completely out of him. Paula and I instantly sprang into action. Before he could recover, Paulo and I wrapped the thief up in several volleyball nets, while Gordon stuffed a stinky old gym sock into the man's mouth. We continued to wrap him in the nets until only his feet showed. Then we tied him up with some skipping ropes and heaved the thief onto his feet.

"Now march!" ordered Gordon, kicking the man in the butt and forcing him to bunny-hop down the hall to the principal's office.

Once there, Gordon phoned the police. "My friends and I have just captured a computer thief in our school," he told them. "We'll hold him in the office until you can get here. And if there's a reward, don't forget to bring it!"

Next, he phoned the local newspaper. "Hello," he said. "My friends and I have just captured a dangerous criminal at Danglemore Public School. With no concern for our own safety and thinking only about the school, we laid a clever trap and caught the computer thief. We're holding him right now while we wait for the police. I guess that makes us heroes. I'm sure you'll want to come over right away and be the first to get the scoop. My friends and I would be happy to pose for pictures."

Meanwhile, the thief started to struggle and moan as he tried to get out of the volleyball nets.

"Shut up, you!" ordered Gordon. "Save your sorry story for the police!"

Seconds later we could hear the sound of sirens as they grew closer and closer. Then the police rushed into the building and ran down the hallway towards the principal's office.

"Where is he?" shouted the Chief of Police, bursting into the room, two officers close behind.

"Right there," said Gordon, pointing to the feet sticking out of the volleyball nets. "Be careful. He's a dangerous one."

"And a fighter," I added, getting into the spirit of the moment.

"Alright. Let's see who we have here," said the Chief, slapping his nightstick against the palm of his hand. As he was untangling the man from the volleyball nets and skipping ropes, the press arrived on the scene.

"Perfect timing," said Gordon. "We're just about to see who the thief is."

And then it happened. As the last of the nets were pulled away from the thief and the stinky gym sock was removed from his mouth, Gordon, Paulo and I stared in shock. The computer thief that we had captured turned out to be none other than our principal, Mr. Evans!

"I knew it!" said Gordon, turning to the police and the reporters. "I always suspected Mr. Evans had a shady side, and this proves it! Book him, boys! Lock him up and throw away the key!"

"I can explain everything!" said Mr. Evans in an angry voice. He pointed into the hallway at a pile of empty computer boxes. "Our school's new computers arrived today and I was working late tonight so that I could get them up and running for the kids on Monday. I heard a strange noise, and when I checked the gym, these three boys attacked me and wrapped me up in nets. Book *them* and throw away the key!"

"Hmm," said the confused Chief. "I think I'll take the four of you to the station. A phone call to the school's superintendent and all of your parents should help me get to the bottom of this. Book all of 'em!"

As the four of us were being led out of the school, the reporter quickly snapped our pictures and said, "This is gonna make a great cover story tomorrow. I just wish I knew who to thank for calling in this great scoop!"

Chapter 6

The Science Fair

In the history of the world, I think Gordon, Paulo and I are the only kids who ever got in trouble for coming in first, second and third in a school science fair. Here's what happened…

A month ago, our principal announced the date for the annual school science fair. He concluded the announcement by saying, "and as usual, participation in the science fair is completely voluntary."

"And as usual," said Gordon, grinning at Paulo and me, "*we* won't be participating."

"Just one more thing," added the principal. "This year, our school science fair is being sponsored by a university, so there will be prizes awarded for first, second and third place. Second and third place winners will each get $500.00, and the first place winner will receive $1000.00!"

"You know," said Gordon thoughtfully, "I think that for the good of science and our school, maybe we *should* participate this year after all." Paulo and I eagerly agreed.

That night, we got together to begin working on our science fair projects. The university's only rule was that entries must be "green," meaning good for the environment. Gordon, Paulo and I each put a lot of thought into our projects. We cared deeply about the prize money, I mean, the environment, and by the time the science fair came we each had excellent entries. We proudly brought them into the school gym for judging.

For my science fair project, I removed the heavy, clunky wheels from my old wagon and replaced them with light, skinny racing wheels. I showed the judges how even the slightest push moved the wagon effortlessly forward because there was less friction between the tires and the ground. I suggested that if we improve the tires on cars like I had done on my wagon, it would save a lot of gas and this would be good for the environment. The three university judges listened to my presentation and nodded their heads. They silently wrote notes on their clipboards. Then they stepped forward to see Paulo's project.

Paulo stood behind two tables. On the first table was a 100 pound pile of fresh, stinky cow manure. The table next to it also held manure – a small one pound pile of dried, odourless cow manure. Paulo explained how his farm uses a windmill to power ultraviolet lights that can dry large piles of smelly manure into compact piles of odourless fertilizer, making things much better for the environment. The three scientists silently nodded and made notes on their clipboard. Then it was Gordon's turn.

Gordon stood next to a huge six-foot high, six-foot wide fan. He explained how he had found this factory fan in the town dump and he and his dad had rebuilt it and turned it into a hyper-velocity fan that was ten times more powerful and yet used 80 per cent less electricity. A fan such as this could keep the entire school cool while drastically lowering electricity costs. Unfortunately, Gordon had forgotten his extension cord at home and was unable to demonstrate the fan's enormous power. Despite this, the judges seemed to like Gordon's project. They smiled and wrote on their clipboards.

That morning, the university scientists inspected over 80 science projects, and after lunch, a breathless Mr. Evans burst into our classroom, pointed at Gordon, Paulo and me, and gasped, "Those three boys did it!"

Alarmed, Mrs. Hoagsbrith said, "Oh, no! What have they done now?"

"Well," began Mr. Evans, pointing at me. "This young man just placed third in our science fair!" Then he pointed at Paulo. "And this fine boy came in second place! And, rather unbelievably, Gordon Smith took first place with his giant fan that uses less electricity!" The whole class applauded and cheered.

"Wait! There's more," said Mr. Evans, waving his hands for silence. "The scientists say that of all the science fairs they've judged this year, these three entries were the best they've seen. Tonight at the awards ceremony, they are going to film a demonstration of the boys' projects so that they can be shown to schools everywhere!" There was more clapping and cheering. Turning to the three of us, he said, "I want you boys to take the rest of the day off and go home and rest up for tonight. The ceremony starts at 7pm sharp, and I don't want anything to go wrong."

Gordon, Paulo and I raced for the door, and spent the rest of the day dreaming about how we would spend our prize money.

At 6:30, we arrived at the school and found the gym packed solid with kids, parents, and a dozen important people from the school board. In the front row with our teacher sat the three scientists and two TV reporters with their film cameras.

At 7:00, a hush fell over the gym. Mr. Evans stepped onto the stage and introduced me. He went into great detail about how I had improved the wagon simply by putting four super-efficient wheels on it. I then demonstrated by giving the wagon a very small push with my fingers. The wagon rolled effortlessly across the stage. There was applause and one of the scientists joined us on stage and presented me with my award and a $500.00 cheque!

I left the stage pulling my wagon and went backstage where Paulo waited his turn. Together, we put his huge heavy pile of manure onto the wagon and when Mr. Evans introduced Paulo, he rolled it easily out onto the stage. Paulo explained how his farm converts piles of stinky manure like the one on the wagon, into small, odourless bundles, like the one he held up. Everyone applauded. The scientist thanked Paulo and gave him his award and cheque.

Paulo ran backstage to help Gordon carry out his huge, supersonic fan. After Mr. Evans introduced him, Gordon went into great detail on how he and his dad had rebuilt the fan to make the extremely powerful fan it now was.

"And now," said Gordon, holding up the extension cord that he remembered to bring, "I will plug it in and demonstrate how quickly this fan will cool the entire gym." He walked to the back of the stage and plugged in the fan. With the roar of a jet engine, the fan leapt to life, drawing warm air into the back and blowing cool air out of the front. And then it happened.

Several feet behind the fan sat my super smooth-gliding wagon, and on top of my wagon was Paulo's science fair project – 100 pounds of fresh, stinky manure! Gordon, Paulo and I noticed it at the same time and we dove for the extension cord to pull it out, but we were too late! In an instant, the wagon was pulled toward the fan, and manure was sucked up and drawn into the back of the supersonic fan. It sprayed out through the front of the fan at a hundred miles per hour, flinging fresh manure across the entire gym! Manure splattered on the walls, ceiling and floor. The lights were covered in it. Worst of all, the entire audience was coated from head to foot in the stuff. Gordon managed to pull the plug, but it was too late. Only Gordon, Paulo and I, who had been behind the fan, managed to escape the deadly spray.

As the noise of the fan died down, we could hear the screams and cries of the audience as a filthy Mr. Evans herded everyone outside. Someone called the fire department, and they arrived with their sirens wailing. The firefighters hosed everyone off until they were clean enough to drive home.

Gordon, Paulo and I were told to report to the office immediately. Mr. Evans stood behind his desk in his dripping wet suit, sputtering at us. "Well, I should have known something like this would happen. Something always goes wrong when you three boys are nearby! Well, I have good news and bad news. The bad news is that the entire gym has to be power-washed and repainted. The good news is, it's going to cost $2000.00, which is exactly how much you kids just won tonight! Now hand it over! And I want each of you to promise me that you will *never* participate in a voluntary school science fair again!"

Chapter 7

To Teacher, With Love

It was the end of June, and tomorrow it would finally be over. Another long school year was coming to an end. For the past few days, teachers had been pretending to teach and kids had been pretending to learn. It was an annual truce which everyone understood would end when the new school year began again in the fall.

Gordon, Paulo and I were out riding our bikes, hoping to find a new fishing spot for the summer. Gordon came to an abrupt stop beside a road we'd never noticed before.

"Hey, I wonder what's down this road?" he said.

"Let's try it and find out," suggested Paulo. "Maybe it will lead to a creek or a lake or something."

It was a fairly boring road, as far as roads went. There were a few farms along the way and a small factory at the very end of the road, which turned out to be a dead end. A sign said, 'Triple A Mining Company.'

"Well," I said, as we turned our bikes around. "That was a waste of time. Now we have to ride all the way back for nothing."

We pedalled in silence for a few minutes, and then Gordon skidded to a stop and yelled, "Hey! Look at this!" He jumped off his bike and started climbing down the ditch at the side of the road. Paulo and I looked at each other and then got off our bikes and followed. At the bottom of the ditch, Gordon reached down and picked up the largest firework I had ever seen. It was almost a meter long and as thick as a baseball bat.

"Wow!" I said. "This is great! What should we do with it?"

"Well," said Gordon. "I know our parents think fireworks are very dangerous and they'd be angry if they caught us with one." Paulo and I nodded in agreement. "So," he continued. "The right thing to do is to light it

ASAP. That way we won't be caught with it and we'll spare our parents the trouble of getting angry."

Paulo and I grinned in agreement. We could always count on Gordon to make doing the wrong thing sound like the right thing to do.

We then began a discussion on where the best place would be to light our giant firework. Gordon snapped his fingers and said, "I got it! Mrs. Hoagsbrith doesn't live too far from here. We could surprise her with her own private firework display, you know, for being such a good teacher and for putting up with us all year."

"That's a great idea," said Paulo. "We can ride over to her house after dark and set it off."

"And we'll leave her a note," I added, "so she'll know who to thank tomorrow!"

"Mrs. H. sure is lucky to have students like us," Gordon said.

Yes, I thought to myself. *This has all the elements of a great idea. First, it will cost us nothing since we found the firework, and second, we might personally benefit from it. Mrs. H. might be so happy that she'll make some last minute changes – positive changes – to our report cards. What could possibly go wrong?*

We headed straight to Paulo's house to write a nice note which we all signed. Paulo took a book of matches that his mother kept safely hidden in the back of the top cupboard, and just before dark, we biked over to our teacher's house.

When we arrived at the woods beside Mrs. Hoagsbrith's house, we hid our bikes and walked the rest of the way along the path behind her farm, staying hidden from view.

We cautiously approached the driveway, where Mrs. Hoagsbrith's brand new pick-up truck was shining in the moonlight. We could hear muffled voices coming from the front porch. It was our teacher and her husband, sitting on their porch swing, enjoying a quiet summer evening. *And it's only going to get better,* I thought.

I snuck around to the back of the house and taped our note on the door, where it would hopefully be found the next morning. Gordon set the firework in the back of Mrs. Hoagsbrith's new truck, and Paulo lit the fuse. Then all three of us ran and dove into the ditch to watch the beautiful display. Gordon quietly counted to 10. We grinned at each other, pleased that we had found such a nice way to honour our teacher. Wouldn't she be surprised!

Just as Gordon finished his countdown, there was a blinding flash of light, and then it happened.

KABOOM!

There was an ear-splitting explosion and the sound of metal being torn apart.

We watched in horror as pieces of Mrs. Hoagsbrith's brand new truck flew a hundred feet into the air. Burning metal and tires rained down around us in the ditch. The windows on our teacher's house were blown in. Smoke got in our eyes and we choked on the stench of burning rubber. It was all over in a few seconds. There was silence except for the crackling of a few small fires. Shaken, but unharmed, we climbed out of the ditch. Gordon, Paulo and I stared at each other. Finally, I whispered what we all knew.

"That was no firework! That was a stick of DYNOMITE!"

"Hey, where did Mrs. H. go?" asked Paulo, very concerned. And then we saw our teacher and her husband dragging themselves out of the flower garden where the force of the blast had thrown them clear off the porch. Fortunately, they weren't hurt, so we figured that the best thing to do was to head home as quickly as possible. Maybe tomorrow we could explain what really happened and tell our teacher how sorry we were for accidentally blowing up her truck.

We decided to take the back roads to Paulo's farm and sneak into the house. With any luck, no one would have even noticed that we were gone.

Coming up the back lane to Paulo's farm 15 minutes later, we saw something that made our blood run cold. Sitting in the driveway were six police cars, and Paulo's father was surrounded by a dozen police officers. The Chief of Police held a piece of paper in his hand and was reading something. Paulo's father suddenly looked up and saw us. Even from this distance, I could see his eyes and his large muscles begin to bulge as he shoved his way through the crowd of police officers to greet us with what Paulo called "old school parenting." Fortunately for us, Mr. Lima was tackled by four cops and wrestled to the ground, where they continued to struggle. The Chief opened up the back door on one of the cruisers and told us to get in. Worried that Paulo's dad might break free, we eagerly dove into the back of the police car. The Chief got into the front of the car and turned to us.

"Okay, boys," said the Chief. "I'm going to give you one chance to explain, and if you don't tell me the truth, I'm going to take my officers back to town and let Mr. Lima handle this for me."

Gordon, Paulo and I decided to play it cool, and between sobs and tears, we blurted out our story. The Chief listened carefully and then sent a patrol car to investigate the dead-end road where we found the dynomite (which we *swore* we thought was a huge firecracker!) Luckily for us, the police found a few more sticks of dynamite in the ditch that we hadn't spotted.

Apparently they had fallen off the back of a truck from the mining company.

Fortunately, the Chief believed our story, and he finally agreed that we had made an innocent (but dangerous) mistake. Mr. Lima finally calmed down and said that he believed us, too.

As the police were leaving, Gordon said, "Chief, I was just wondering. How did you find out it was us?"

"Oh, that was easy," replied the chief. "Don't you remember? You left your teacher a note."

"The note!" we yelled, remembering. "Oh, no!"

The Chief reached into his pocket and pulled out the slightly burnt note. It said: "Dear Mrs. Hoagsbrith. "Words can't describe how we truly feel about you, so we thought we'd show you instead. We hope you enjoy our little surprise."

Chapter 8

All You Can Eat

It was the middle of summer, and so far, Gordon, Paulo and I had seen four movies at the theatre and spent countless hours playing computer games. Now we were stretched out in front of the TV in Gordon's living room enjoying our favourite show. Just then, Gordon's mother entered the living room and said, "Gordon, I want you and your friends to go to the grocery store for me. Here is the list…"

"Shhhh," said Gordon, waving his hand dismissively, not even looking up from the TV. "My show is on."

In the blink of an eye, our show was *off*, and we were hurrying down the street with Mrs. Smith's shrieks still ringing in our ears.

"Wow!" I said. "Your mom can sure move fast."

"Yeah," agreed Paulo. "And she sure can yell."

"Yes," said Gordon. "I must say, for an old girl, I keep her in pretty good shape."

When we returned with the groceries, we discovered that the 'old girl' had been busy. She hung up the phone, looking pleased with herself, as we entered the kitchen.

"There! It's done," she said smugly.

"What's done?" asked Gordon suspiciously.

"Well, your birthday is in less than a week and I just phoned everyone who's coming to your party and told them that they are not allowed to bring any toys or games as presents."

"Great!" exclaimed Gordon. "They're all bringing money instead?"

"Of course not!" said his mother. "I told them that you were spending far too much time playing games and watching TV, and not enough time reading, so they are all giving you books."

Gordon gasped in shock and fell to the floor in a dead faint. Stepping over him on her way out of the kitchen, Mrs. Smith told Paulo and me to take Gordon upstairs for a little rest.

As soon as Gordon's mom left the room, Gordon miraculously recovered and began moaning. "Books for my birthday? What a waste of a year!"

*   *   *   *   *

Four days later, Paulo and I arrived at Gordon's party. I brought a book that my aunt had given me last Christmas. It was still wrapped in its original Christmas wrapping paper, complete with a Christmas card still in the envelope. I had crossed out the part that said *Merry Christmas* and wrote *Happy Birthday, Gordon* instead. I handed it to Gordon who looked at it and noticed the little Santas and elves. "Thanks," he said sarcastically. "You shouldn't have gone to so much trouble."

"No trouble at all," I assured him. "It was my pleasure. Oh, and let me know if it's any good so I can tell my aunt."

In the end, of all the books that Gordon received that day, the only one that looked even half interesting was a book from Paulo called 'Eat Or Be Eaten: Your Guide to Surviving in the Wilderness.' We spent a few days taking turns reading each chapter aloud, and we felt like wilderness survival experts by the time we were finished.

"Boys," I said, "if a pack of wolves ever attacks our school, we'll be the only survivors." We grinned with pleasure at the thought.

Now that we were experts on wilderness survival, we decided that it was time we went on our very first wilderness canoe trip to put our new skills to the test. The only problem was getting past our mothers, who had always forbade us to go canoeing on our own.

"It's too dangerous," my mom would say.

"You'll get lost," Paulo's dad would say.

"You could be killed by a pack of wild animals!" Gordon's parents would say.

Today, however, luck was on our side. Our mothers had recently drawn straws to see which two got to go away for a few days and which one had to stay home to watch Gordon, Paulo and me. Gordon's mother had drawn the short straw so she had to look after us. We found her lying on the living room sofa with the curtains drawn, a cold cloth on her forehead, and a drink in her hand. We burst into the living room to tell her of our latest plans.

"Hey, mom!" shouted Gordon excitedly. "Can we go on a canoe trip for a couple of days?"

To our surprise, Mrs. Smith raised her head and said, "Tell me about it and we'll see."

"Well," said Gordon. "It's totally cool. You drop us off at a place called Tumbling Timber Falls and we spend the next three days paddling our canoe down these huge rapids and portaging around waterfalls. Then, in about four days, you pick us up at a place called Bail-Out Bridge."

We all crossed out fingers and waited. Finally
Gordon's mom said, "No. It's too dangerous. You could
be killed, and what would the neighbours think?"

We sadly turned to go when Gordon spotted his dad
pulling into the driveway from work. Mr. Smith burst into
the house yelling, "Honey, where are you? I've got some
great news!"

"I'm in here," called Mrs. Smith wearily. Gordon's
dad burst into the room. "Hey, guess what happened at
work today? My boss had to cancel his vacation at the
last minute and he gave me two free tickets to… wait for
it… *Adult Land Resort!* We can leave first thing in the
morning!"

Gordon's mom pointed to Gordon, Paulo and me. "We
can't go," she said sadly. Gordon's dad frowned, seeing
his plans evaporate before his eyes. That's when Gordon
piped up.

"Gee," he said. "If only we could get out of your hair
for a few days so you could go on your wonderful
vacation to Adult Land."

"No!" said Gordon's mom, not fooled for a minute. "You're not going on that canoe trip. It's far too dangerous."

"You're probably right," said Gordon. "So maybe we could come with you on your vacation!"

"Absolutely not!" said Mrs. Smith firmly. "It's called *Adult Land* for a reason. And remember what happened the last time we took you three boys on vacation with us?"

"That's too bad," said Gordon's dad. "Did I mention that the vacation includes a free ladies' day at the spa and a $500.00 shopping spree?"

"Tell me again about this canoe trip, boys," said Mrs. Smith, sitting up. "Maybe a few days of exercise and fresh air are just what you need. I'll help you pack!"

Early the next morning, Gordon's parents dropped us off at Tumbling Timber Falls. I dreaded this part, where Gordon's parents would no doubt rhyme off a huge list of do's and don't's and tell us a hundred times to be careful. Gordon's dad would make us promise to wear our life jackets at all times, and then Gordon's mom might even try to kiss us good-bye. But much to my surprise, as soon as the canoe was off the car and our packs were unloaded, Gordon's parents jumped back into the car and sped off down the road without even so much as a quick wave or a backward glance.

Before the dust settled, we had the canoe loaded and in the water. We pushed off and began paddling down the river. The current was pretty strong, and we were making such good time that in a couple of hours, we decided to slow our paddling down and just let the current carry us along. We shut our eyes for a little rest, and before we knew it, we were fast asleep. Several hours passed, and then it happened. I was jolted awake by the sound of rushing water! The riverbank sped by and our canoe was being carried along at an alarming rate.

"Wake up!" I shouted to Gordon and Paulo. "Get the map! How far ahead is Dead Man's Falls?"

Gordon rummaged around in his pack. "I can't find the map!" he shouted. "We must have forgotten it!"

I glanced ahead and noticed water smashing into rocks and then disappearing over a large waterfall…Dead Man's Falls! The last thing I remembered was a beautiful rainbow over the falls, but I knew there was no pot of gold at the end of this one! In an instant we were swept over!! The canoe crashed down and smashed into rocks. Packs were flung over the sides. We took on wave after wave of water and our canoe promptly sank, taking what was left of our food and supplies with it! Gordon, Paulo and I were swept downstream and when we were finally able to get out of the current and crawl to the shore, we were bloodied, bruised and out of breath.

"I can't believe it!" I gasped, coughing and spitting out water.

"Me neither," said Paulo. "It happened so fast!"

"What kind of parents would send their kids on such a dangerous canoe trip just so they could have a lousy free vacation?" shouted Gordon. "My grandparents are gonna hear about this!"

"*If* we survive," said Paulo gloomily.

"What do you mean, *survive*?" I asked. "Just open up that book to the chapter on being swept over a waterfall and losing all of your equipment."

Paulo pointed to the middle of the river. "It's out there somewhere, with all of our other gear."

"Well," said Gordon. "I'm never going to read a book again. Look at the kind of trouble it gets you into. There should be a warning label on books!"

After much thought and discussion, we figured we were about 60 miles from home and decided to get walking.

It wasn't long before darkness came and night set in. We curled up along the riverbank and spent the night, hungry and shivering. The next morning, we awoke early and continued our journey homeward. We were weak with hunger and our mouths drooled at the thought of food. We spent another hungry, cold night in the great outdoors, and by about noon on the third day, we stumbled out onto a dirt road. That's when we knew we were saved! Sooner or later, a car would come by and rescue us!

It turned out to be later, not sooner. Two hours went by and not a single car had passed. We were dead tired and starving. Gordon suddenly snapped his fingers and pointed at the roadside. "Look! We're saved!"

"What?" said Paulo and I at the same time.

"Grass!" cried Gordon, delighted. "Grass!! Remember? That survival book said you could eat grass and survive!"

In seconds, the three of us were down on our hands and knees tearing up the grass and gulping it down. It tasted terrible, but we didn't complain. We were so busy wolfing down grass that we didn't hear the small sports car pull up beside us and stop.

"Hey, boys! Watcha doing?" a man hollered at us.

We jumped to our feet and immediately saw the grocery bags that were stuffed into the tiny car, filling the passenger seat.

We quickly explained what had happened and that we were so hungry we were eating grass to survive.

"Well, then today's your lucky day, boys," the man exclaimed. "I just live a mile or two up the road. I'd give you a lift, but you can see my car's full of groceries. Just follow the road a ways to my house, and it will be all you can eat!"

Those were the sweetest words I had heard in a long time. *All you can eat.*

Gordon, Paulo and I staggered after the car like drooling zombies. In 20 minutes we crawled up the man's driveway and collapsed at his door. Gordon somehow found the strength to knock, and the man rushed outside and jumped into his car. Laughing, he pointed to his front lawn, which was almost a foot high.

"There you go, boys! You're going to love it, and remember, it's *all you can eat*!" And he sped off down the road.

Chapter 9

The Sea Monster

For as long as I can remember, Gordon's uncle Herman has been saving for a new boat. Uncle Herman always kept his money safely hidden at the bottom of an old rusty toolbox at the back of his garage. Now that he was recently married, he kept the money hidden in an old rusty *locked* toolbox at the back of his garage.

"Yup," he explained to us as he unlocked the toolbox and began counting his money. "I feel kinda bad keeping all this money a secret from my new wife, but not half as bad as I'd feel if she found out about it and wanted to spend it on something foolish like a new kitchen or something for the baby." Gordon's uncle had recently become a dad for the first time. "I shudder to think what my wife would do if she found this stash." With that, Uncle Herman resumed counting. "Eleven hundred, twelve hundred, thirteen hundred dollars! At last I can buy the boat I've been dreaming about since my first marriage."

"Not so fast, mister!" cried a voice from the doorway. Uncle Herman's new young wife stepped into the garage, carrying a baby. "You just keep on dreaming. We need this money to buy things for little Herman Jr. And *I* happen to know a thing or two about *men*. Men with young families don't get to buy new boats!" With that, she grabbed the money out of Uncle Herman's hands and marched out of the garage. A few minutes later we watched as she backed out of the driveway and headed for the mall to go shopping.

Poor Uncle Herman looked sick with the sudden loss of his money, so sick that he barely had the strength to fill his glass with the special medicine he kept safely hidden in the woodpile. The medicine took effect quickly and after a couple of minutes, Uncle Herman put down his glass and said, "See, boys. It's just like I told ya's. I felt bad keeping that money a secret from my wife, and now I feel *twice as bad* that she found out about it! The only good news is that I have the next 4 days off and I'm going to go fishing every day. Help me load up my old boat."

We spent the next few hours helping Uncle Herman get his old boat and trailer ready and just as we were almost finished, his wife pulled into the driveway with a van full of new baby items. "Great news, honey!" she called out. "After all the baby shopping, there was still some money left over."

Uncle Herman broke into a hopeful grin. Maybe there would be enough money left for a smaller boat!

"So," she continued, "I booked a family vacation! We're going to spend the next 4 days at a Clown Resort! Doesn't that sound exciting? Just imagine – 4 days of non-stop clowns. Little Herman Jr. is going to love it!"

I looked at Uncle Herman's face as he imagined four days of non-stop clowns, and I could see his sickness returning. Before I could run to the woodpile for some more of his medicine, his wife said, "Oh, I almost forgot. There was still a bit of money left over after paying for the vacation, so I bought you a present, honey." She handed Uncle Herman a long box and headed into the house to change the baby. Uncle Herman set the box on his workbench and opened it with a knife. He took off the lid and eagerly peered inside. Immediately, his face fell.

"I wanted a new 18-foot fishing boat and she got me a silly remote-control submarine. What is a grown man supposed to do with a remote-control submarine?" He trudged over to the woodpile and dug out his medicine. After a few sips, he perked up again. "Hey, you boys want a submarine?"

Gordon, Paulo and I looked at each other.

"Sure!" said Gordon. "Thanks, Uncle Herman!"

"Enjoy it, although what you kids will do with it, I don't know."

We rushed over to Gordon's house and began reading the instructions on how to use the sub. We soon realized that a remote-control submarine wasn't as exciting as it sounded. You pushed a button and the sub dove to the bottom of a lake or pool. You pushed another button, and the sub surfaced.

"Not that much fun," said Paulo.

"Boring," I agreed.

"I'm not so sure," mused Gordon. "I agree that taking this sub down to the beach would be boring, but what about taking a sea monster to the beach instead? Imagine a huge, man-eating sea monster surfacing in the middle of all those swimmers?" He grinned at us.

"Ha! That would be hilarious, but what sea monster?" I asked.

"Yeah, that would be a lot of fun," agreed Paulo. "Too bad we can't actually do that."

"Oh, but we can!" laughed Gordon. "I've got it all figured out. Remember that huge plastic alligator my mother puts on the front lawn every Halloween to scare people? We'll use that!"

"Won't your mother mind us using her Halloween decoration?" I asked.

"Of course not!" said Gordon. "She's not even home."

We ran to the garage and dug out the Halloween decorations. "Here it is!" said Gordon, looking pleased with himself.

We worked quickly to attach the alligator to our new sub. When we were finished, it actually looked like a pretty convincing sea monster, if you didn't look too close. We hid our sea monster in a huge garbage bag and headed to the beach.

It was a beautiful, warm, sunny day and there were lots of people when we arrived. Most of the kids were little and stayed close to shore where their mothers could keep an eye on them. A few older kids ventured further out into the lake. After surveying the scene for a few minutes, Paulo suggested that we launch our sea monster from a little island in the middle of the lake.

"We can hide in the bushes and no one will spot us," he explained.

We circled around to the other side of the lake and hid our bikes. Then, making sure no one was watching, we took our sea monster out of the box and swam to the island.

"Okay," said Gordon, taking command. "We'll launch the monster from the far side of the island where there are no swimmers, and then use the remote control to bring it around the crowded part of the lake."

"Aye, captain," said Paulo, saluting.

We launched our sea monster and Paulo quickly brought the sub around the island. From our hiding spot behind a clump of bushes, we waited as the sea monster sank to the bottom of the lake and headed toward the swimmers. After a few minutes, Paulo worked the remote control and a giant sea monster popped up, right in the middle of a group of teenagers.

Instantly, the teens began screaming and yelling and swimming as fast as they could toward shore and away from the sea monster. Their shouts alerted everyone else at the beach, and panic broke out! Mothers ran into the water to grab their kids, and a few people on shore began snapping pictures of the sea monster.

"Take her down," commanded Gordon.

"Aye, aye, captain," said Paulo, and the monster slowly sank from view.

We watched as the parking lot cleared out. Kids hopped on their bikes and pedalled off, anxious to tell everyone about the sea monster at the beach. Word quickly spread through town, and within ten minutes, every man with a fishing boat pulled into the parking lot, anxious to get out on the water and capture the creature.

We stayed low, hiding behind the bushes on the island, but despite our cover, we were spotted by two men in a boat.

"Hey!" they yelled at us. "What are you three kids doing?" The men shut off their engines and waited for our answer.

I knew we had been caught and was just about to admit everything when Gordon stood up and shouted back, "*Three kids?* Heck, there were *five* of us in the water a couple of minutes ago!"

All at once, every boat started up again as the men, now truly scared, raced back toward shore. Boats crashed into each other and men toppled out into the water.

"This is getting even better," laughed Gordon. "Surface!"

Paulo brought the sea monster back up.

"Attack!" hissed Gordon, and the sea monster began chasing the men in the water. Not wanting to be the next one eaten by the horrible sea monster, the men doubled their efforts and swam furiously toward shore. Just as the sea monster got close to one man, Gordon ordered Paulo to take the sub down, and our creature disappeared below the surface.

The men had now all made it safely back to dry land, but the lake was strewn with smashed up, burning boats. Several were starting to sink, and Gordon, Paulo and I sensed that this was a good time to make our getaway. We crept out of the bushes, but before we could slip into the water and disappear, we were spotted by the men on shore.

"NO! STAY ON THE ISLAND! DON'T GO INTO THE WATER!! WE'VE CALLED IN THE MILITARY AND THEY'LL COME RESCUE YOU!"

The military?? Gordon, Paulo and I froze. We'd learned recently just how eager the military was to fight UFOs, and we figured they'd be just as keen on fighting a sea monster, especially one that had supposedly devoured two kids.

Trapped on the island, Gordon, Paulo and I sat and waited to be "saved" by the military. Half an hour later, they arrived. It was worse than we imagined.

We watched in fear as a large ship was backed down the boat ramp. It bristled with cannons and missiles. It began to patrol the lake. We stared as six barrels were launched into the air. Just before the barrels splashed into the water, we noticed the words DEPTH CHARGES written on their sides. Instinctively, the three of us dove into the sand began to count down.

"5-4-3-2-1!"

KABOOM!!

The entire island shook. The explosion blasted water and fish hundreds of feet into the sky and a few seconds later, fish and water began raining down upon us. Enormous waves splashed against the shore. For several minutes, it was like being inside a small tsunami. Several more minutes went by before the lake began to calm down. The men on shore seemed to have lost interest in the sea monster and had begun frantically filling every available bucket with the free fish that had been blown ashore. Gordon, Paulo and I waited silently and watched. And then it happened.

The explosion must have disturbed our sea monster at the bottom of the lake, and it slowly began to make its way to the surface. First the head emerged, and then the long tail rose up. The military men aimed their weapons at the monster, awaiting orders. And then, catching sight of the submarine that was taped underneath the monster, they all lowered their weapons. One man reached into the water with a long pole and hooked the monster, hauling it aboard.

Meanwhile, back on shore, the men were still joyously filling their buckets with fish. The captain looked at the fake sea monster and then at the fisherman.

"Those fishermen tricked us!" yelled the captain of the military ship. "They *wanted* us to blow up the lake so they could get all those free fish!"

Angered at not being able to fight a real sea monster, the captain turned his ship toward shore to force the fisherman to put the fish back into the lake. Fights soon broke out, and Gordon hissed, "Quick! Now's our chance to get away!"

We quietly slipped into the water and swam toward the opposite shore, where we grabbed our bikes and headed for home.

"I wouldn't want to be those fishermen right now," panted Paulo.

"If only Uncle Herman's wife had let him buy that boat in the first place, none of this would have happened. It just goes to show you how much trouble a wife and baby can cause!"

And Then It Happened

·· 12 ··